Jocelyn's Cloud

Story by Kaelyn Clementz
Illustrations by Tia Caffee

Published in 2020, by Coco Publications

Coldwater, OH 45828

Kaelyn Clementz

Jocelyn's Cloud

Story by Kaelyn Clementz / Illustrations by Tia Caffee

ISBN

978-1-5323-8772-2

Library of Congress Control Number

2020909302

PRINTED IN THE UNITED STATES OF AMERICA

~Dedicated to my parents for having me, God for giving me life and my Grandmother Patricia for inspiring me to write this book and teaching me how to write a book.

For all the love given to me by family and friends, I am gratefully appreciative.

To my brothers and sisters whom have gone before me, Angel, Thaddeus, Elijah, and Jacob who are peeping down through the clouds at me and cheering me on.

Preface:

Around the first week of March in 2018, I saw a staircase in a cloud. The cloud had made a ring. A dove was inside the ring. Rays were shooting out of it. I believe I was seeing heaven and that Jesus was showing it to me. That is what inspired me to write this book.

~ Kaelyn Clementz

Before I begin my story, I wanted to share with you some advice.
Keep learning. It is endless and your wisdom keeps expanding.
Remember that your elders know a lot and are happy to help
you experience life in unique ways.
Listen when they talk, they can inspire you.

Here are some great facts about clouds.

They are a collection of tiny droplets of water.

There are different types of clouds.

The highest clouds in the atmosphere are cirrocumulus, cirrus, and cirrostratus. Those are some pretty big names for something so natural and amazing!

Status means layer and refers to the group of clouds that form in big sheets covering the entire sky. Cuddle up in this blanket!

Cumulus means heap. These are the clouds that we often say look like bunnies or giant castles. Have you ever seen a bunny in a cloud?

Looks like a big cotton ball. So soft.

Alto means middle. These are clouds that are in the middle layer of the atmosphere.

Cirrus means curl. Those clouds are high up and look like wisps of hair.

Nimbus means rain. When there is precipitation present in those clouds, they are called nimbus.

Mid-level clouds include altocumulus and altostratus.

The lowest clouds are stratus, cumulus, and stratocumulus.

Clouds are white because their water droplets or ice crystals are large enough to scatter the light of the seven wavelengths (red, orange, yellow, green, blue, indigo, and violet), which combine to produce white light.

Clouds and precipitation are due to rising air. As air sinks, its temperature rises and its capacity for holding vapor increases. Then any cloud droplets tend to evaporate and the cloud disappears; evaporation changes moisture back from liquid to gas.

On with the story...

When my grandmother, Patricia, was a child, she would look up at the clouds to see what she could see in them. She had a lot of fun doing this. There was no Internet, so you had to make your own fun. That's what she wanted for me and that's how I got started checking out the clouds.

Try it. Stare at the clouds. What do you see? You might see a face, a dove, or a stairway to heaven. Looking at them and using your imagination, the possibilities of what you see are endless.

The most interesting cloud I saw was one shaped like a face. I could see eyebrows, sunglasses, a nose and mouth. It was funny, but awesome! Tell other people so they might experience what you are seeing. You just might hook them on watching clouds too.

Being outside can be a wonderful experience. Nature is all around, with all kinds of birds, especially eagles. There are deer, cattle, butterflies, fireflies, dragonflies, ponds with fish, and more. Check out the rivers and creeks. Sometimes wildlife will swoop down into the water to catch food to eat. Don't forget the trees, clouds, sun, moon, and stars.

My grandparents live on a farm called "The Broken C, Oasis Farm". While an oasis is usually found in the desert, it can also mean a place of safety and relaxation. On "The Broken C, Oasis Farm" there is a woods with trails for four-wheeling. Wow! So much to see and enjoy!

If we were up in the clouds, we could play peek-a-boo by making some clouds into people. Then we could play hide-and-seek by making walls and certain figures. As you lay back and watch the clouds, write or draw with your fingers in the sky.
There are artists who do this.

The long strip clouds can become slides to go from one cloud to another. Or they could be a trampoline to jump to the next cloud. How high can you go?

Climb a mountain. Some clouds have peaks, like mountains. Your imagination has no limits. Your imagination becomes your friend. No fears up there and you can be on vacation all the time.

Hopefully you will bump into an angel on the way. You might have a white dove land on your shoulder or a butterfly. Now relax and daydream!

Have a dive from one cloud to another. I would like jump into a cloud, sleep on a cloud, spend the night with stars at my side on a cloud. Wouldn't that be an awesome and unforgettable experience? The clouds look so soft, white, and fluffy.
Wishing they could be my mattress.

Have you watched the clouds on a windy day? It seems like they are moving at a high rate of speed. They go left and right. One cloud on top of another sometimes. Putting on my sky diving get-up suit to dive from the top cloud to the bottom cloud.
Wow! That was an amazing jump!
Remember, we are just playing make believe.
WEEEEEEE!

It's a different experience when you watch the clouds turn gray, which usually means a storm is coming. Watching the sunset and sunrise around clouds is incredible too.

Another day when you are playing make believe, imagine being up there and touching the pot of gold at the end of a stunning rainbow. Who knows, you might see a leprechaun as well. Explore!

Since I told you about clouds, I will tell you what makes a rainbow. A rainbow is a spectrum of light that appears in the sky when sunlight is refracted through rain drops in the earth's atmosphere.

The slide we built might come in handy if we run into a rainstorm. We must be prepared at all times. The slide will take us home in a hurry. You can dream a dream. This one is with clouds. Now relax and let's daydream. No stress, just complete relaxation.

My father and mother saw a cloud shaped like a heart on the way home from my dad's grandfather's funeral. Like I said, keep looking. You never know what you will see.

Lots of clouds can look like an entire city. We might want to bring some color along to bring the city to life. We need some lights in the city as well to differentiate the sky scrapers we have created. Have you ever heard of the rock and roll song, "We Built This City on Rock and Roll" by Starship? My grandmother told me about that song.

Make a school building out of a cloud so you can attend there. Make a helicopter out of a cloud too to get to that school. No buses here!

What shapes and images have you seen in a cloud?

Some clouds we have seen are the backside of a large lion.
We also seen a whale, an octopus, a polar bear, all white of course.
And we've seen Dumbo the elephant sitting and laughing.
We've seen a blue gill, too.

Another time, we clearly saw a dog shaped cloud with ears flopping
back, tongue out. It looked like he was running. Breezy!
Was it Cloudy, my dog's name in this book?

I've seen an eagle, the Hulk, a dragon, and a fox terrier. Even more incredible, I've seen a Care Bear running, a mammoth gorilla, and Winnie the Pooh. Of course, there are many other things too, like a large platform with a smaller one below it. Was it a stage? I've seen a crucifix and a woman with a scarf over her head, holding a baby. I have seen an alligator, whale, yellow duck. Remember the kind we use to take our baths with? I have seen the Jetson's space ship.

What about the alphabet? Have you seen any letters?
I once saw a C shaped cloud. I've seen an A, Z, E, and X.
What about numbers? I have seen the number 3. Make sure
you look quickly because clouds can move and change shapes
very fast. Have you seen any states? I saw the state of Utah.
Isn't this fun?

Live on a cloud by making a huge mansion out of it with a swirling stairway. Invite people to come to visit and have fun. You will need a pet. Make a puppy out of cloud and name him Cloudy.

"Let's Go Surfin'" by the Beach Boys would be a good song to listen to while you stare up at the clouds. That's another song my grandmother told me about.

I have seen a tunnel shaped cloud. On another day, in that tunnel, ride a ride like Sir Richard Branson from the TV show "Shark Tank" is making through space travel. Wow! Astonishing! I wish I would have invented that. Can you imagine going into space through his space travel program. It would be as much fun as my day dreaming trip in the sky. Right?

It is all what you make of it.

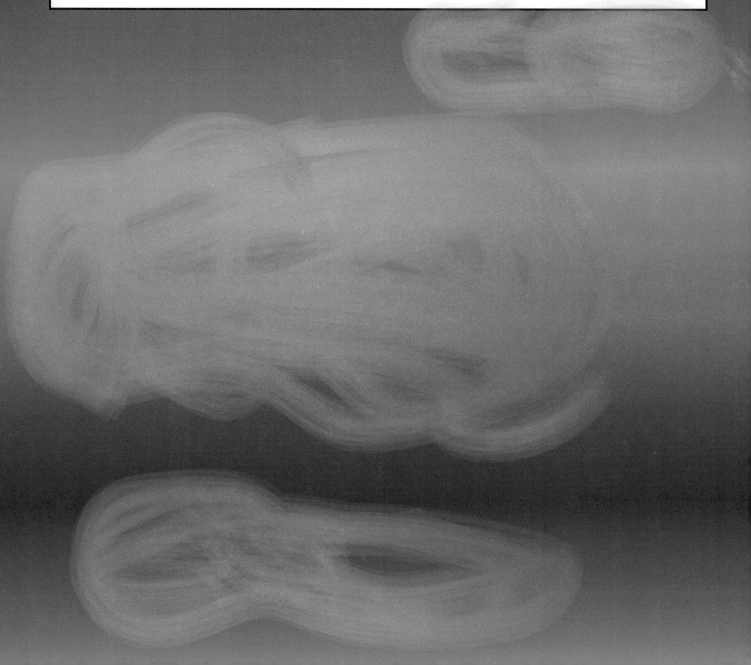

My grandparents say, "Watch the clouds when they are really dark and low. The sky looks wicked. A storm is on the way or brewing somewhere."

I hope this book has inspired you to go on a cloud adventure.
Life is a gift. Enjoy it and be creative.

Have you heard the saying, "Every cloud has a silver lining?"
The saying means every difficult situation will eventually get better.
Just like the dark clouds that pass when the sun comes out.

So do clouds really have a silver lining? The bright outline along the edge of the cloud is the silver lining, which occurs when light is diffracted by cloud droplets. That's another interesting fact.
I hope you're enjoying learning this cool stuff.

I was with my grandmother on July 3, 2019. We were discussing if we thought we could add to the book or if it was finished. My grandmother was in the car when she saw a rosary shaped cloud. She saw beads in the cloud; there were 3 with the cross at the end. We discussed it and thought this was a sign that the book was now finished or at least we were on the right track with the story.

The great thing about writing is you never stop thinking and adding. Well, on the 4th of July celebration my grandparents said God was having his own fireworks. There was a cloud, actually two clouds side by side in the sky. There was heat lightning going on the whole time inside the clouds, while the fireworks display was going on. It was so neat. Be grateful that you can see such magnificent displays.

While I'm at it, I might as well say that on days when there aren't many clouds, check out the sky. It might have a lavender hue. It might be what's referred to as sky blue, blue-green, violet, aquamarine, royal blue, Egyptian, teal, cornflower, azure, sapphire, Carolina, Steel, tiffany, Turkish blue, turquoise, powder, or cerulean.

Lastly, never stop learning. Just like these shades of blue, you would be surprised how many different colors have different names because of slight differences in the shade. The great cosmos. The place of humankind in this great universe. Keep seeing, believing, and dreaming.

I bet tonight you will be looking at the sky seeing what you can in the clouds. Remember to look often. The clouds are different every day and you will see a lot in your lifetime. It is beautiful.

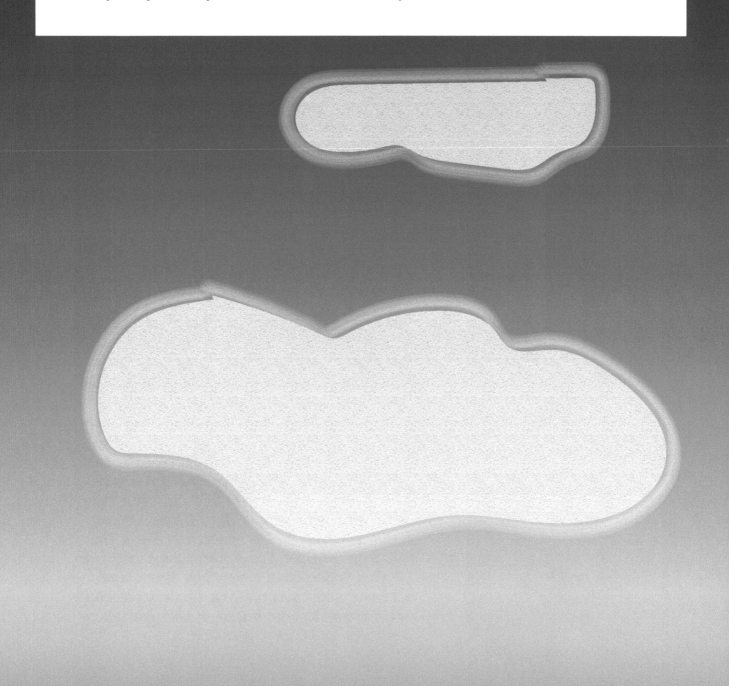

About the Author

Kaelyn is a country girl who loves to read. She was in the talented and gifted program for reading in school. She loves the outdoors and nature such as taking walks, riding her golf cart, biking, swimming, looking at the clouds, sky, moon and especially the stars. She's an animal lover especially dogs and cats and some day hopes of having pet horses and goats. She's also athletic and loves basketball and volleyball. She was taught to value family and friends.
Kaelynn was 11 years old when she wrote this book and is now 12.

About the Illustrator

Tia Caffee is a graduate of Parkway High School and studied Graphic Design at Wright State University-Lake Campus in Celina, Ohio. She loves to draw in various mediums. Tia is the daughter of Jon and Lisa Caffee, the younger sister to Caleb Caffee and the proud aunt to Rilynn, Maci, Dierks and Caden Caffee. She is also the author of The Oasis, Brothers of the Art, Divine, Maria: Witch in Training and Hindered. She's the illustrator to Billy Joe Boomershine and the Toilet Paper Bandit by Judy Bruns and Daelynne and Lauren Make Applesauce and Daelynne and Lauren's Day in the Garden by Jeremy Wenning.

CPSIA information can be obtained
at www.ICGtesting.com
Printed in the USA
LVHW070551201120
672145LV00002B/20